D0581844

Teachers, librarians, and kids from
across Canada are talking about the
Canadian Flyer Adventures.
Here's what some of them had to say:

Great Canadian historical content, excellent illustrations,
and superb closing historical facts (I love the kids'
commentary!). ~ *SARA S., TEACHER, ONTARIO*

As a teacher–librarian I welcome this series with open
arms. It fills the gap for Canadian historical adventures
at an early reading level! There's fast action, interesting,
believable characters, and great historical information.
~ *MARGARET L., TEACHER–LIBRARIAN, BRITISH COLUMBIA*

The *Canadian Flyer Adventures* will transport young
readers to different eras of our past with their appealing
topics. Thank goodness there are more artifacts in that old
dresser ... they are sure to lead to even more escapades.
~ *SALLY B., TEACHER–LIBRARIAN, MANITOBA*

When I shared the book with a grade 1–2 teacher at
my school, she enjoyed the book, noting that her students
would find it appealing because of the action-adventure
and short chapters. ~ *HEATHER J., TEACHER AND
LIBRARIAN, NOVA SCOTIA*

Newly independent readers will fly through
each *Canadian Flyer Adventure*, and be asking for
the next installment! Children will enjoy the fast-paced
narrative, the personalities of the main characters, and
the drama of the dangerous situations the children
find themselves in. ~ *PAM L., LIBRARIAN, ONTARIO*

I love the fact that these are Canadian adventures—kids should know how exciting Canadian history is. Emily and Matt are regular kids, full of curiosity, and I can see readers relating to them. ~ *JEAN K., TEACHER, ONTARIO*

What kids told us:

I would like to have the chance to ride on a magical sled and have adventures. ~ *EMMANUEL*

I would like to tell the author that her book is amazing, incredible, awesome, and a million times better than any book I've read. ~ *MARIA*

I would recommend the *Canadian Flyer Adventures* series to other kids so they could learn about Canada too. The book is just the right length and hard to put down. ~ *PAUL*

The books I usually read are the full-of-fact encyclopedias. This book is full of interesting ideas that simply grab me. ~ *ELEANOR*

At the end of the book Matt and Emily say they are going on another adventure. I'm very interested in where they are going next! ~ *ALEX*

I like when Emily and Matt fly into the sky on a sled towards a new adventure. I can't wait for the next book! ~ *JI SANG*

A Whale Tale

Frieda Wishinsky

Illustrated by Dean Griffiths

MAPLE
TREE
PRESS

Maple Tree Press Inc.
51 Front Street East, Suite 200, Toronto, Ontario M5E 1B3
www.mapletreepress.com

Text © 2008 Frieda Wishinsky   Illustrations © 2008 Dean Griffiths

Distributed in Canada by Raincoast Books
9050 Shaughnessy Street, Vancouver, British Columbia V6P 6E5

Distributed in the United States by Publishers Group West
1700 Fourth Street, Berkeley, California 94710

Dedication
To my friend Margaret Litch, remembering wonderful days on Vancouver Island and more to come!

Acknowledgements
Many thanks to the hard-working Maple Tree team—Sheba Meland, Anne Shone, Grenfell
Featherstone, Deborah Bjorgan, Cali Hoffman, Dawn Todd, and Erin Walker—for their insightful
comments and steadfast support. Special thanks to Dean Griffiths and Claudia Dávila for their
engaging and energetic illustrations and design.

Cataloguing in Publication Data
Wishinsky, Frieda
A whale tale / Frieda Wishinsky ; illustrated by Dean Griffiths.

(Canadian flyer adventures ; 8)
ISBN 978-1-897349-16-8 (bound). ISBN 978-1-897349-17-5 (pbk.)

I. Griffiths, Dean, 1967– II. Title. III. Series: Wishinsky, Frieda.
Canadian flyer adventures ; 8.

PS8595.I834W43 2008   jC813'.54   C2008-900424-8

Library of Congress Control Number: 2007939085

Design & art direction: Claudia Dávila
Illustrations: Dean Griffiths

We acknowledge the financial support of the Canada Council   ONTARIO ARTS COUNCIL
for the Arts, the Ontario Arts Council, the Government   CONSEIL DES ARTS DE L'ONTARIO
of Canada through the Book Publishing Industry Development Program (BPIDP), and the
Government of Ontario through the Ontario Media Development Corporation's Book Initiative
for our publishing activities.

Printed in Canada
Ancient Forest Friendly: Printed on 100% Post-Consumer Recycled Paper

A   B   C   D   E   F

CONTENTS

HOW IT ALL BEGAN

Emily and Matt couldn't believe their luck. They discovered an old dresser full of strange objects in the tower of Emily's house. They also found a note from Emily's Great-Aunt Miranda: "The sled is yours. Fly it to wonderful adventures."

They found a sled right behind the dresser! When they sat on it, shimmery gold words appeared:

> Rub the leaf
> Three times fast.
> Soon you'll fly
> To the past.

The sled rose over Emily's house. It flew over their town of Glenwood. It sailed out of a cloud and into the past. Their adventures on the flying sled had begun! Where will the sled take them next? Turn the page to find out.

Grey Whale
Friendly Cove, West Coast
Spring 1778

1

I Wish

"I wish you could ride a whale," said Emily. "My friend Trish saw whales last summer in British Columbia, and she brought me this book about them. Look at this picture!"

Emily picked up a book from her desk. She showed Matt a photograph of a whale leaping in the ocean.

Matt laughed. "Imagine riding a whale. It would be amazing!"

"It would also be slippery. I wish I could see whales this summer instead of going to

Grandma's cottage. Of course, there are no whales on her lake, just beavers."

"I like beavers. They build terrific dams," said Matt.

"But whales spout water like a fountain!" said Emily. She showed Matt a photograph of a whale doing just that.

"That picture is awesome!" said Matt. "Maybe the magic sled could fly us to a whale adventure. Let's go to your tower and check it out."

Emily and Matt raced up the rickety stairs to the tower. As soon as they were inside, Emily headed for the mahogany dresser. She opened the top drawer. They peeked in.

"No whale stuff here," Emily said.

They opened the second drawer. "None here either."

They opened the third drawer. "Nuts,"

said Emily. "Nothing! There's no whale stuff anywhere."

"Wait," said Matt. "There's a wooden carving in the corner of the drawer. I think it's a... whale! Yahoo!"

"What does the label say?"

"*Grey Whale, Friendly Cove, West Coast, Spring 1778.*"

"How high do grey whales leap?" asked Emily. "I hope they spout water like crazy, and we get soaked. I can't wait to draw a picture of *that*."

"And I can't wait to record whale sounds. I have my recorder in my pocket. Do you have your sketchbook?"

Emily patted the pocket of her jeans. "It's right here, like always."

"Let's go!" Matt pulled the Canadian Flyer sled out from behind the dresser.

Emily and Matt hopped on. Shimmery gold words appeared immediately.

Rub the leaf
Three times fast.
Soon you'll fly
To the past.

Emily rubbed the maple leaf three times fast. Instantly, thick fog enveloped the sled. When the fog cleared, they were flying.

"Whale adventure here we come!" she called as they flew over her house, over their town of Glenwood, and into a fluffy white cloud.

"Hey, Em," said Matt, as they headed out of the cloud. "What if we land on a whale, and then it dives under? What if we can't get off in time?"

"Don't worry. We probably won't land *right* on a whale."

"We are! Look down there!" cried Matt. "It's a huge grey whale, and we're heading right for it!"

2

Slimy

The sled flew down toward the gigantic creature.

Matt held his breath. Emily clutched the sides of the sled so tightly that her knuckles were as white as the blotches on the whale's sides.

"Please, please turn, sled," Emily prayed. Emily and Matt leaned forward. They tried to steer the sled away from the whale.

But the sled kept going down, down, down. The water was still. Suddenly the great whale

came shooting up out of the sea. It heaved its huge body nearly all the way out of the water, then fell sideways with a giant splash.

"Look!" cried Emily.

A boy in a canoe was paddling near the whale.

As the whale breached again, the canoe began to tip in the waves. The boy tried to keep it steady, but the canoe rocked wildly.

The sled dipped lower. They were so close now that they could almost touch the whale's rough skin.

"We're all going under!" shouted Matt. He shut his eyes. He could almost feel the icy water.

But he didn't.

"Matt!" cried Emily. "Open your eyes. We're safe! The sled just turned. We're heading for shore."

"Hurray!" shouted Matt as the sled landed on a pebbly beach.

"Phew," said Emily. "We almost did ride a whale, and if we had, we'd be under the sea by now. My heart is still pounding. I hope the boy in the canoe made it to shore safely."

"Let's get off the sled and look for him," suggested Matt.

They slid off the sled. The beach felt cold and bumpy under their feet.

"Hey, we're not wearing shoes. Ouch!" cried Matt. "These rocks are sharp on my bare feet."

"I'm getting pebbles between my toes," said Emily.

"I am too," said Matt. "But we'd better hide the sled, so we don't have to explain to anyone what we're doing with a sled in the spring."

Matt picked up the sled and looked around for a good hiding spot.

"How can we have an adventure without shoes?" groaned Emily. "My feet hurt."

"We don't have a choice," said Matt. "We'll have to get used to it. And we'll have to get used to these itchy clothes." He rubbed the loose top and pant-like bottoms he was wearing.

Emily sniffed the material. "This smells like our cedar closet! Someone wove strips of wood together to make these clothes. This is one crazy adventure. No shoes and clothes made of wood!"

"But I bet it will be fun. Come on! There's a big rock over there. Let's hide the sled behind it and cover it with seaweed."

Emily made a face. "That seaweed looks slimy. I don't want to touch it."

"And no one else will want to touch it either," said Matt, pushing the sled behind the rock. "That should keep the sled safe and hidden.

Let's cover it quickly before anyone sees us and then go look for that boy."

Emily and Matt quickly covered the sled with seaweed.

"One more slimy piece should do it," said Matt.

Emily peeked out from behind the rock. "I see someone coming. Over there!"

Matt peered out. "It's the boy from the canoe. He's safe!"

They watched as the boy climbed up on a large boulder. He sat down, crossed his legs, and began carving a piece of wood. Then he began to sing.

3

Tuta

"I wonder what he's singing, and what he's carving?" said Emily. "Let's go talk to him."

"What if he saw us flying on the sled? How can we explain *that*?"

"We'll think of something," said Emily. "Come on. We can't stay here forever."

Emily and Matt headed toward the boulder.

"Ouch!" cried Emily. "I cut my foot on a rock."

The boy spun around.

He was wearing an outfit like theirs, and he was barefoot too.

Emily stumbled up the boulder. She sat down and inspected her foot.

"Is it bleeding?" asked Matt.

"Yes," said Emily.

"I will help," said the boy. He scrambled off the boulder and ran to the trees near the shore.

"Phew!" said Matt. "I don't know what language that boy is speaking, but we understand it. And he understands us too."

"Good old magic!" said Emily. They watched the boy pull a plant out by the roots and hurry back.

"Here," he said. "This will make your foot feel better."

He used a rock to break up the leaves and flowers of the plant and gave it to Emily. "Just hold it against your foot. Soon the bleeding will stop."

"Thanks," said Emily. "How can you walk barefoot around here? Don't your feet get cut up on the rocks?"

"I know where to step, and my feet are as hard as these rocks. Where are you from?"

Emily and Matt glanced at each other. What could they say?

"We're from...far away," said Matt. "My name's Matt, and this is Emily."

"I am Tuta, nephew of Chief Maquinna."

"Your uncle's the chief! That's awesome," said Matt.

"What were you singing?" asked Emily.

"I was calling to the grey whale. I was thanking it for not tipping my canoe today. I was close to the whale when it breached. It sprayed so much water, I could hardly see, and then my canoe began to tip. But before it did, the whale swam away."

"Do you always paddle in the ocean by yourself?" asked Matt.

"No. This was the first time. I wanted to prove to my uncle that I could, so he would let me join him on the next whale hunt. He says I am too young, but I am not."

Emily gulped. "Don't people kill whales on a whale hunt?"

"We only kill whales for food. Whales are special to us. We honour their spirit and thank them for the gift of food they bring to our village."

Tuta held up his carving.

Emily and Matt couldn't believe it. It was the whale carving that they'd seen in the dresser!

"It's beautiful," said Emily.

Tuta smiled. "I am almost finished with it."

"Is that your uncle?" Matt pointed to a tall

man coming toward them. He wore a long flowing cape and a cone-shaped hat.

"Yes," said Tuta. "I have not seen him for days. Not since the big ships came."

"What ships?" asked Matt.

"Men from far away have come here with their chief, Captain James Cook."

"I've heard of him!" Matt whispered to Emily as Tuta stood up to greet his uncle. "He's a famous explorer."

"Tuta, I have been looking for you," said Chief Maquinna. "I saw you take the canoe out alone today. You must never do that again. It is dangerous."

"But nothing bad happened, Uncle. I came back safely."

"You were lucky. Now go and help your mother prepare for the potlatch."

The chief glanced over at Emily and Matt.

"Who are these children?" he asked.

"They are my new friends, Matt and Emily," said Tuta.

Chief Maquinna smiled at Emily and Matt. Then he turned to Tuta again. "Your friends can help you prepare for the potlatch. Remember, tonight we celebrate the birth of your baby sister. I have invited many villages. There will be dancing, much food, and many gifts for the guests. And there is much to do."

"Please, Uncle," said Tuta. "I can do more than help prepare for the potlatch. I want to go on the whale hunt. I am not a child."

Chief Maquinna put his arm around his nephew. "You are too young and inexperienced, Tuta. Enough talk. Run to the longhouse and help your mother. She is waiting."

4

Fish *Again!*

Emily and Matt followed Tuta down the beach.

"My uncle doesn't understand," grumbled Tuta as he led them toward a long building made of enormous cedar logs. "I am not a child. I faced that whale today, and I can do it again. But all he wants me to do is help with the potlatch."

"The potlatch sounds like a big birthday party," Emily whispered to Matt as they neared the longhouse.

"It sounds like fun," said Matt. "Look!"

Matt pointed to two huge totem poles standing in front of the long building. Emily and Matt peered up at a figure of an animal-like creature carved into one of the poles.

"It looks angry," Emily said.

Tuta laughed. "Do not worry. It is not angry. The totem just identifies our clan and name."

The children stepped inside. Baskets, mats, wooden boxes, food, and people filled the long building.

"Who lives here?" asked Emily.

"My family and my uncle's family," said Tuta.

Tuta led them to a rear corner of the building where a woman was sitting on a mat and rocking a baby, and a man was working on a carving that looked like a wolf mask.

"Mother, Father. These are my friends, Emily and Matt. They have come to help me prepare for the potlatch."

"Your mask is amazing," said Emily to Tuta's father. Tuta's father smiled.

Tuta's mother looked up. "Tuta, there are

many fish to clean for tonight's celebration." She pointed to a basketful of shiny salmon in a corner.

"Oh no," whispered Emily to Matt. "I don't want to clean fish."

"You do not like fish?" asked Tuta as they picked the basket up and headed out to the beach.

"We like eating fish, just not cleaning them," said Matt. He glanced at Emily. Emily rolled her eyes. They both remembered how much they hated cleaning fish when they had explored with the Vikings.

"Please help. There are so many fish," said Tuta. "I will never finish it alone."

Matt and Emily sighed. They wanted to help Tuta. He'd helped Emily when she'd cut her foot on the rock.

"Sure," said Matt. "We'll help."

The three children sat on a rock, gutting and cleaning fish.

"I wish I was in a canoe instead of cleaning fish," said Tuta.

"I wish I was doing *anything* except cleaning fish," said Emily.

A Surprise Gift

"Finally!" exclaimed Matt after they'd cleaned the last salmon.

"I don't want to clean another fish ever," said Emily.

Tuta picked up the basket of fish. "Wait here! I will take this back to my mother. Then I will show you a good place to see whales from the shore."

As Tuta ran off, Emily sniffed her hands. "My hands stink of fish," she said. "Let's wash up in the ocean."

Emily and Matt waded into the water until their ankles were covered. They bent over and washed their hands.

"Brrr... This water is as cold as ice cubes," said Emily. "Let's get back to shore."

They hurried back to wait for Tuta.

"Wasn't that wolf mask Tuta's father was carving awesome?" said Matt. "I wish we could try on one of those masks."

"Maybe we can! Look what Tuta's carrying!"

Tuta was running toward them with his father's wolf mask. "My father just finished it! I know how much you liked it, so I wanted to show you."

Tuta handed the mask to Emily and Matt. "I have to bring it right back, but first I have to get another basket of fish."

"More fish," moaned Emily. "I thought we were finished."

"It is just a small basket," said Tuta as he ran off. "We will finish quickly, and then I will show you the whale place."

"I bet it took hours to carve this," said Matt, examining the mask.

"Let me try it on," said Emily.

"Sure," said Matt.

Emily placed the mask against her face. "How do I look?"

"Fierce. Let me try it on too."

Matt held the wolf mask against his face. Then he crouched down, jumped around, and howled like a wolf.

"What do you think you are doing?" bellowed a voice.

Matt stood up. Oh no! It was the chief. He was coming toward them and waving his fist! And right behind him, Tuta was running toward them too.

"We're…just…," stammered Matt as Chief Maquinna approached.

"Emily! Matt!" called Tuta.

Chief Maquinna spun around and glared at Tuta. He wagged his finger at his nephew. "Was this your doing?" he demanded. "You know that the wolf masks are sacred. They are not for children to play with. How can I trust you to join the whale hunt, if you permit your friends to treat the masks with disrespect?"

Tuta's face turned red. He gulped. "Uncle…," he began. "I…I…"

"Please, Chief Maquinna," Emily chimed in. "It wasn't Tuta's fault. He didn't know we'd try it on. We just thought the mask was amazing. We've never seen anything like it."

"And we didn't know the mask was sacred," said Matt.

"Uncle, Emily and Matt are from another

village," said Tuta. "They do not know our ways. Do not be angry with them. They meant no harm."

For a minute, Chief Maquinna said nothing. He just looked at the three children.

Then his face softened

"Perhaps if I were a child," he said, "I would want to try such a wonderful mask on too, but that is not our tradition. You must never do this again."

"We promise," said Emily and Matt.

"Now I must return to the longhouse. I will take back the mask. It is needed for tonight's dancing." And with that, Chief Maquinna left.

Emily flopped down on the beach. "Phew," she said. "Chief Maquinna was really angry."

"But you helped him understand, Tuta. Thanks!" said Matt. "We didn't want you to get into trouble."

Tuta took a deep breath. "When I saw my uncle's face, I was sure he would never forgive me. And if he did not forgive me, I would never have a chance to join the hunt. But he understands now."

"So where's the basket of fish?" asked Emily.

"My mother asked my cousin to clean those fish. No more for us!"

"Hurray!" cheered Matt and Emily.

"And look! There's a whale!" Tuta pointed out to sea.

Emily and Matt looked up.

They didn't see anything. But then, after a minute or two, they saw a giant grey whale's back slide through the water near the shore. Its wide, flat tail just broke the surface as it dived again.

"I have never seen a whale so near to this

spot before," said Tuta. "I wish I could paddle close to it right now. They come up quietly right beside you," he added, "and you can look into their eyes."

"Wow! Imagine looking into a whale's eye!" said Emily. "I wonder what they think when they see us?"

"I am sure they understand us. They are clever creatures. We tell stories about them at festivals like the potlatch. We also dance at the potlatch. Do you like to dance?"

"I do," said Emily.

"I don't. I'm not good at dancing," said Matt. "I trip on my own feet."

"I dance a lot. I take ballet lessons," Emily explained. "I'll dance with you, Tuta."

"What is ballet?" asked Tuta as they headed back to the house.

"It's a dance you do on your toes, like this."

Emily stood up on her toes and did a little pirouette.

"Ouch!" she cried. The pebbles on her bare feet made her stumble. "That wasn't graceful. It's hard to pirouette on pebbles." Emily rubbed her feet and laughed.

"That is a very strange dance," said Tuta. "We do not stand on our toes and spin. We stamp our feet and jump around like this."

Tuta stamped his feet and leaped into the air. He landed on the pebbles without falling or wincing in pain.

"That's awesome," said Matt. "I wish I could do that."

"You can. I'll show you how," said Tuta. "You will like dancing. It is fun."

6

The Potlatch

Tuta, Matt, and Emily hurried back into the longhouse.

Inside, the cedar mats were covered with baskets of food.

"Look at all this food," said Matt.

Tuta pointed at each basket and said, "Fireweed. Salmonberries. Strawberries."

Matt whispered to Emily, "Some of these look like weeds. If I knew they liked weeds here, I would have brought a bucketful from home."

"I'm not eating weeds, but I'll try the clams

and mussels. And I'll even have a piece of salmon," said Emily.

"Well, I'm not eating the octopus." Matt grimaced at a pile of octopus in a basket. "Should we taste everything to be polite, Tuta?"

"Eat only what you wish," said Tuta, laughing. "But we hope you will eat lots. That is part of the potlatch tradition. We want our guests to enjoy all the special food we have prepared. Listen! The music is starting!"

People began to beat drums and shake rattles. Others wearing wolf masks began to dance round the longhouse.

"Come! Dance with me here!" shouted Tuta. He pointed to a spot to the side of the main group of dancers.

"I'm ready!" said Emily, spinning around.

"I'm not," said Matt. "Like I said, I'm really not good at dancing."

"I will show you," said Tuta. "Watch me and do the same. You can dance. It is not hard."

Emily and Matt watched Tuta. They copied all his movements. They danced for what felt like hours.

"Hey! This is fun!" said Emily, at last. "But I'm out of breath. This is even harder than ballet!"

Emily flopped down on the ground.

"It *is* fun," said Matt. "But how can you do this for so long? My legs ache. I have to sit down, too." Matt sank down beside Emily.

"See! You both danced well," said Tuta, as the drums stopped. "Now follow me. It is time for the gift giving. You can sit with my family."

Tuta, Matt, and Emily hurried to the spot where Tuta's family was seated.

Chief Maquinna strode to the front of the whole group. About one hundred people had gathered.

"What's going to happen now?" Matt whispered to Tuta.

"My uncle will hand out the gifts," said Tuta. "It is the most important part of the

potlatch. You might even receive a gift today."
Tuta winked at his friends.

"We get a gift even though we tried on the mask?" said Emily.

"My uncle is kind. I am sure he is no longer angry."

"Awesome!" said Matt. "I just hope our present is not a fish."

"It's better than a fish," said Tuta. "I wish I could be given a gift for the potlatch. But my family is giving the potlatch, so I cannot receive a present."

"What would you want?" asked Emily.

"To join the whale hunt. It is the only thing I want."

Chief Maquinna approached Matt and Emily.

"Tuta, you must give your friends their special gift." Chief Maquinna handed Tuta a small wooden object. Tuta smiled as he held it out to Matt and Emily.

Emily's eyes widened. "It's your whale carving!"

"It's beautiful. Thank you," said Matt.

Tuta beamed. Then the chief handed out gifts of baskets, boxes, and food to the other guests. While Chief Maquinna circled the longhouse, Emily and Matt examined Tuta's carving.

"It looks just like the grey whale we keep seeing," said Matt.

"Maybe we'll look that whale in the eye, yet," said Emily. "Imagine if you could hold onto reins on a whale like a horse. What a wild ride that would be. It might look like this."

Emily pulled out her sketchbook and drew a picture of the two of them holding reins and riding a whale.

"Giddy-up, whale!" said Matt, laughing.

"Hey, Tuta!" Matt looked around for his friend. "Where's Tuta? He was here a minute ago."

Emily glanced around. "Maybe he took a walk on the beach to see the whale again. He keeps talking about it."

"You don't think he's planning to take the canoe out again tonight?"

"I hope not," said Emily. "But he might. He really wants to prove to his uncle that he can join the hunt. If he goes out now, pretty soon he'll be stuck out there in the dark."

"Come on, Em. Let's hurry and find Tuta before he does anything crazy like that!"

A Decision

Emily and Matt raced toward the beach.

They peered around. They called his name.

"I don't see him. Do you?" said Emily.

"There's the canoe, way down the beach," said Matt. "I can't tell from here if Tuta's in it."

Matt and Emily hurried to the canoe.

But Tuta wasn't there.

"Do you think he took another canoe?" asked Emily.

"I don't know, but I'm worried. It's a cloudy night, and he'd be paddling without much light from the stars or the moon. It could be really dangerous. What do you think we should do?"

"Let's look around the beach a little more," said Emily.

Matt and Emily walked slowly along the beach. They looked up and down, but it was hard to see anything.

"We'd better head back before we get lost," said Matt. "Maybe Tuta is back from wherever he went and is waiting for us. Maybe he's worried about us!"

"No he's not," said Emily. "There he is! Up on that rock, looking out to sea."

Emily and Matt scrambled up the large, jagged rock. "Tuta!" they called.

Tuta turned around and waved.

"We were worried about you," said Emily.

"I was here the whole time. I needed to think," said Tuta. "I have decided."

"What have you decided?" asked Matt.

"I will take the canoe out to sea tomorrow and find the grey whale. I must prove that I am ready for the whale hunt. I know my uncle will change his mind when he sees I have gone out to sea again and come back safely."

"He's going to be angry. He told you not to go alone," said Matt.

"That's why you must come with me. Please? It will be a wonderful adventure. You like adventures, don't you?"

Emily and Matt laughed. "We love adventures," they said.

"So you will come? Please?" begged Tuta.

Matt and Emily looked at each other.

Tuta was determined to go out to sea. How could they say no to him? How could they let him go out alone? How could they miss seeing the grey whale from a canoe?"

"We'll come," said Emily.

Tuta beamed. "Wonderful! Tomorrow morning. We leave at dawn. You must stay at our house tonight, if my family and your family agree."

"I'm sure we can stay," said Matt.

"But you'll have to wake us in the morning," said Emily. "I'm not good at waking up early."

"I will wake you, but we will have to slip out quietly, before anyone sees us!"

"We'd better get back now," said Emily. "I don't want to walk on pebbles in the dark."

The children climbed off the rocks and walked carefully back to the longhouse.

"I can't believe it," said Emily, when they arrived. "My feet hardly hurt this time. I'm getting good at walking barefoot on rocks!"

Soon they stretched out on cedar mats in the longhouse.

"Don't forget," whispered Tuta. "We leave at dawn."

"Goodnight," said Matt yawning. "I'm so tired."

"Me too," said Emily, closing her eyes.

Emily tried to sleep, but she kept picturing them in the canoe beside the whale. What if, this time, the whale made the canoe *really* tip over? Could they swim in the icy water? Could they reach the shore in time?

Emily tapped Matt on the shoulder. "Are you asleep yet?" she asked.

"Almost," muttered Matt.

"Do you think we'll be safe in Tuta's canoe? Maybe it's dangerous to get too near a whale."

"Tuta knows how to paddle. He knows the sea. He made it back safely before. And we said we would go with him. Don't worry so much, Em. Go to sleep." Matt turned over.

"I hope you're right," said Emily. "But Matt, what if..."

Matt was fast asleep. And soon, so was Emily.

8

Dawn

Before she knew it, Emily felt someone shake her gently. It was Tuta.

"Wake up. It's time."

Emily opened her eyes. She stretched. "It can't be dawn already," she said. "Just give me five more minutes to sleep. Then I'll get up."

"We must go now. Not later," insisted Tuta.

Tuta shook Matt. Matt opened his eyes.

"It is dawn," whispered Tuta. "You both must get up *now*. We must go before anyone wakes."

Matt and Emily sighed and scrambled out

of bed. Emily grabbed the whale carving. "I'm taking this along for good luck."

The children moved past Tuta's parents and his baby sister. No one stirred. They walked past another family. The father was snoring loudly, but everyone was sound asleep.

They tiptoed on, and then Matt tripped on a basket of dried fish. He stumbled to the ground.

"Ouch," he said, and he groaned.

"Shh," whispered Tuta, bending over to help him stand up. "Are you hurt?"

"Not much," Matt whispered back.

The children tiptoed toward the entrance to the longhouse. But just as they headed out, Tuta's baby sister began to cry.

"Run!" whispered Tuta. Emily, Tuta, and Matt raced outside. As they made their way toward the beach, they heard Tuta's sister wail once more, and then she was quiet.

"Phew," said Matt.

"I hope she didn't wake anyone," said Emily.

"We cannot worry about that now," said Tuta. "Hurry! The sun is rising."

The children raced to the beach.

"Look! It's a perfect day for an ocean adventure!" sang Tuta. "The ocean is as calm as a pond. Come on!"

The children followed Tuta to the canoe. Tuta hopped on and steadied the canoe as Emily and Matt took their places carefully. Emily placed the carving in her lap.

Tuta's eyes sparkled as he pushed the canoe into the water. "Today we will see the grey whale. Today I will prove to my uncle that I am ready for the hunt."

Tuta paddled the canoe into the bay. Emily and Matt peered around. They saw mountains thickly covered with trees. Tuta pointed out small islands inhabited only by birds. They watched sea otters floating together in the kelp beds. They heard birds squawk and fly overhead.

They scanned the sea for the grey whale, but they didn't see a sign of it anywhere.

They drifted out farther as the sun rose and warmed their faces. Still no sign of the whale.

"It must be here," said Tuta. "We are close to where I spotted the whale yesterday."

"Are those Captain Cook's ships?" asked Emily as two great ships sailed around a point and came into view.

"Yes," said Tuta. "We trade with Captain Cook and his men."

They waved to three sailors who were cleaning the deck of the nearest ship.

The sailors waved back. Then one of them

leaned over the rail of the ship and shouted.

"What is he saying?" asked Tuta. "I do not understand his words. Do you?"

"I can't hear him," said Matt.

The man shouted again. He made a face and pointed out to sea.

Another sailor joined the first sailor. Both men signaled to the children to look behind their canoe.

Tuta turned his head. A baby grey whale was swimming close to the canoe. And right behind her, an enormous grey whale was advancing swiftly. The large whale lifted her huge head out of the water and smashed down onto her side.

"Oh, no!" cried Emily. "Do you think we're too close to the baby?"

"Yes," said Tuta. "We must not let her think we will harm it. We must get out of here fast."

A Whale Tail

Tuta began to paddle quickly away.

The enormous whale swam closer and then breached again, covering the children with spray and making bigger waves. The canoe rose and fell, and then it rocked from side to side. Tuta couldn't make it stop.

"Help! We're going under!" yelled Matt.

"We can't go under," moaned Emily, clinging to the side of the canoe.

"Look! Cook's ship is sailing toward us. Maybe they're coming to help!" shouted Matt.

"Hold on. Do not be afraid. We will not tip over," said Tuta. But despite his brave words, sweat poured down his face. He paddled with all his might, trying to straighten the canoe. It rocked and tipped, but finally he steadied the canoe.

Tuta wiped his face with the back of his hand. He sighed with relief.

"I don't see the whales anymore," said Emily, scanning the ocean. "Maybe they've gone. Maybe we're safe. Maybe... Oh no!"

The mother grey whale was back! She surfaced next to the canoe, nudging it with her great body.

Emily and Matt clung to the sides of the canoe as it tossed and turned in the churning water.

"Do not be afraid. We will get out of here," said Tuta. Spray drenched his face and clothes.

His hands were wet and slippery, but he clung to the paddle. He dipped it over and over into the choppy water.

"Please don't tip us over, beautiful whale!" cried Emily.

"W...we don't want to harm you or your baby," stammered Matt. A wave rolled into the canoe. Emily, Matt, and Tuta screamed and tumbled forward. The carving flew out of Emily's lap and over the side.

"Oh no!" Emily cried. "The carving fell overboard!"

Tuta quickly reached out for it, but it was too late. The carving floated away like a toy boat.

And then both the mother and baby whale turned and swam away.

Emily sat back in the canoe. She took a deep breath. "I have never, ever, been so scared," she said.

Tuta wiped sweat and ocean water off his face. He stopped paddling. "The whale heard your words," he said. "She knew we meant no harm."

"But I lost your carving," said Emily.

"Perhaps the carving was good luck. Maybe its sacrifice helped save our lives," said Tuta. "Maybe it is not even lost. Maybe it will float back to shore."

Emily smiled. Tuta was right, although of course he couldn't know why. The carving wasn't lost because it was in the dresser in her tower room.

"Well, whatever made the whales swim away is fine with me. We were almost goners," said Matt.

"Your amazing paddling saved us, Tuta," said Emily.

"Emily's right," said Matt. "If you hadn't paddled so well and stayed so calm, we would have tipped over. You kept us upright."

"It is good we were together, but we should head back now. I have had enough adventure for one day," said Tuta. "I'm just glad my uncle did not see us."

"Tuta," said Emily, pointing to shore. "Your uncle *did* see us! He's standing on the beach with your mother and father. I think Captain

Cook is with them. At least he *looks* like a captain."

Tuta's face turned white. He gulped. "Oh no," he groaned. "I am in big trouble. This time my uncle will surely not forgive me, and my parents will be angry too. My uncle will never let me join the hunt now."

No one said anything as Tuta paddled the canoe toward shore. When they reached the beach, the children dragged the canoe out of the water.

Chief Maquinna, Tuta's parents, and Captain Cook were waiting for them.

10
When?

Tuta swallowed hard. He faced his uncle and parents. "I...I...am sorry. I wanted to prove to you that I could paddle skillfully. I did not expect the grey whale to come so close."

"You and your friends almost drowned," Tuta's father scolded him.

"It is all my fault," said Tuta. "I asked my friends to come with me."

"But Tuta saved us," said Matt.

"He was amazing," said Emily. "He is the best paddler in the world. He stayed calm all the time, even when the whale was almost inside the canoe."

Captain Cook pointed out to sea toward the spot where the children had encountered the whale. The captain smiled and patted Tuta on the back.

"Well done," he said.

Emily and Matt knew that Tuta and his family didn't know English, so they couldn't understand Captain Cook's words. But it was clear from the captain's warm smile that he thought Tuta was brave.

"Well, Tuta. You are lucky," said his uncle. "I was certain your canoe would tip over. You kept your head and your paddle. You were foolish to go out with your friends, but you were brave. Perhaps some day soon you can join us on the hunt."

"Really?" said Tuta. "When, Uncle?"

"Perhaps next year," said Chief Maquinna.

He put his arm around his nephew. "Yes. I think you will be ready in just one more year."

"But, Uncle, I am ready now. I am not a child. I will listen to everything you tell me on the hunt. I will help you. You will see. I—"

Chief Maquinna threw his head back and laughed. "All right, Tuta. I can see that you are brave *and* determined. I like those qualities in a young man, but if I allow you to join the hunt this year, you must heed every word I say."

"I will! I will!" said Tuta, jumping up and down. "This is the best present I have ever received! I'm going on a whale hunt!"

"Let us return to the longhouse now," said Chief Maquinna.

"Come. Help me with your sister, Tuta," said his mother.

"Will you come too?" Tuta asked Emily and Matt.

"Soon. We need to check on something first," said Matt.

Tuta waved and headed back to the long-house with the adults.

"Come on, Em. Let's make sure the sled is still there," said Matt "I hope no one found it."

Matt and Emily raced to the rock where they'd left it.

"Good old slimy seaweed," said Emily, laughing. "It's where we left it, and so is the sled."

Emily lifted a long strand of seaweed off the front of the sled. As soon as she did, words began to form on the front of the sled.

You've helped a friend.
You've seen a whale.
It's time to fly
And end this tale.

"The sled wants us to go home," said Emily.

"But we have to say goodbye to Tuta," said Matt.

"I'll leave him a picture. I'll leave it on the boulder where he always sits. He'll wonder where we went, but at least he'll have this picture to remember us by. I hope he'll always remember that we were friends."

"Hurry!" said Matt.

Emily quickly sketched Tuta waving from the canoe, smiling at the grey whale and her baby.

Emily dashed to the boulder, put the picture on it, and placed a big rock on top to hold it down. Then she ran back to the sled.

"Jump on!" said Matt. "The sled is moving!"

Emily hopped on the sled. Immediately the sled lifted off the ground. It flew above the beach and the ocean.

"Look!" said Matt. "There's the grey whale and her baby!"

The two whales were swimming and breaching side by side. As they did, both whales blew a fountain of water out of their blowholes.

"Wow!" cried Matt. "That was..."

"Awesome!" shouted Emily.

Matt laughed, pulled out his recorder, and spoke into it. "We're flying over the ocean. There's an awesome grey whale and her baby below us. We have had an amazing adventure."

Before Matt could say anything else, the sled flew into the fluffy white cloud. And soon after that, Emily and Matt landed back in the tower room.

"Hurray! The slime is off the sled!" said Emily sliding off.

"And our shoes are back on our feet," said Matt, tapping his heels.

"Are you hungry?" asked Emily. "We never had breakfast."

"I'm starved," said Matt.

"Good. Let's go to your yard and get some weeds. It will be delicious with scrambled eggs."

"It will not," said Matt.

Emily laughed. "I know. Let's have toast instead."

MORE ABOUT...

After their adventure, Emily and Matt wanted to know more about the Nootka, whales, and Captain Cook. Turn the page for their favourite facts.

Matt's Top Ten Facts

1. The Nootka people prefer to be known as the Nuu-chal-nuth. Captain Cook called them Nootka because he didn't understand them. When the people first paddled out to Cook's ships, they called out, "Itchme nutka, itchme nutka," which really meant, "Go around, go around."

> The Nuu-chal-nuth were pointing out a better harbour, not introducing themselves! -E.

2. Hunting whales is dangerous and difficult. Only skilled Nuu-chal-nuth people were allowed to hunt.

3. A whaling canoe usually carried eight whalers. The chief owned the canoe and the whaling equipment.

4. Because whales are so large and their skin is tough hunters had to get close to plunge in the harpoon.

5. The harpooner sat at the front of the canoe. His harpoon was made of yew wood and a mussel shell.

6. The side of the canoe was curved inward to prevent water from getting in the boat and sinking it.

7. When the harpooned whale was finally brought to shore, everyone met it as an honoured guest.

8. Grey whales migrate the same way year after year. They spend the winter around Baja, Mexico, and swim north up the coast to what is now British Columbia, where they stay from March to May. The grey whale's 16,000 km (9,940 mile) round trip is one the longest of any mammal.

9. For many generations, the highest-ranking chief in Nuu-chal-nuth society was given the name Chief Maquinna.

10. The secrets of whaling were passed down from father to son. Only when a boy was old enough to understand how to be a whaler, was he allowed to join the hunt.

Emily's Top Ten Facts

1. In Nuu-chal-nuth villages there were three groups of people: chiefs, commoners, and slaves. The chiefs owned the slaves..

2. The Nuu-chal-nuth people changed locations with the seasons. They moved to Yuquot (Friendly Cove) for the spring and summer, when there were lots of fish, water, birds, seals, whales, and sea otters.

3. When it started to rain in late August, they moved inland and caught salmon.

Fish! Fish! Fish! I bet they would have liked a p.b. & j. sandwich for a change! —M.

4. In November, the families moved to their more inland winter home. They hunted deer and bear, and they fished. By late December, they went to the coast fishing for herring.

5. Red cedar was used by the Nuu-chal-nuth to make many useful objects such as hats, clothes, mats, and baskets. Red cedar is strong and light, and doesn't rot.

Good. I wouldn't want to wear rotten clothes. —M.

6. Usually women gathered shellfish such as clams, mussels, abalone, oysters, and periwinkles.

7. Dishes were hollowed out of blocks of alder, which didn't spoil the taste of food. Spoons were made of mountain goat horns and wood.

8. The Nuu-chal-nuth often decorated their hats with scenes with whales.

9. The Nuu-chal-nuth are kind to their children. They never spank them.

10. You could tell that a chief or a noble Nuu-chal-nuth was important by how much they gave away at a potlatch.

So You Want to Know...

FROM AUTHOR FRIEDA WISHINSKY

When I was writing this book my friends wanted to know more about the Nuu-chal-nuth and Captain James Cook. I told them that *A Whale Tale* is based on historical facts, but all the characters except for Chief Maquinna and Captain James Cook are made up. Here are some other questions I answered:

How did James Cook become an explorer?

James Cook started out as a servant aboard a ship in 1746. For eight years, he sailed on different ships around England. When he was 26, he joined the Royal Navy. People soon recognized that he was a skilled seaman and he was quickly promoted. In 1758, he sailed to Canada and excelled at surveying and map making. The English government recognized his skill and commissioned him to explore unknown lands.

Where did he go on his first voyage as captain?

In 1768, Cook embarked on his first voyage aboard the ship HMS *Endeavour*. The main reason for the trip was to visit Tahiti and observe the planet Venus as it passed by the sun. The measurements would be used to help sailors navigate. Another purpose for the trip was to explore new lands in the Pacific.

Was this trip successful?

In many ways this three-year trip was a great success. Cook circumvented the globe in a westerly direction. He also brought back many unusual plants from around the world. But disease killed many important crewmembers, including botanists (who studied plants), artists, astronomers, and sailors.

What was Cook like as a captain?

Cook cared about his men. He cared so much that he made them eat sauerkraut (cabbage preserved in brine) and lime juice, which he thought would fight a terrible disease called scurvy. He was organized, tried to keep the ship clean, and was tough with sailors who disobeyed his orders (he flogged them).

How did Captain Cook meet the Nuu-chal-nuth?

On March 29, 1778, Cook's ships *Resolution* and *Discovery* anchored along what is now Vancouver Island in British Columbia. The local people paddled over, chanting a welcome to the strangers. Their greeting, their long houses, and totem poles impressed Cook. He repaired his ships in the harbour and traded with the people.

Where did Cook sail next?

The *Resolution* and *Discovery* sailed to what is now Alaska, Siberia, and even crossed the Arctic Circle. Then they headed to Hawaii. Unfortunately, while repairing the ships, Cook and a few members of his crew got into an argument with the Hawaiians and were killed.

Coming next in the
Canadian Flyer Adventures Series...

Canadian Flyer Adventures
#9

All
Aboard!

Ride the rails with Matt and Emily
in this thrilling railroad adventure.

The *Canadian Flyer* Adventures Series

#1 Beware, Pirates!

#2 Danger, Dinosaurs!

#3 Crazy for Gold

#4 Yikes, Vikings!

#5 Flying High!

#6 Pioneer Kids

#7 Hurry, Freedom

#8 A Whale Tale

Upcoming Book

Look out for the next book that will take
Emily and Matt on a new adventure:

#9 All Aboard!

And more to come!

More Praise for the Series

"[Emily and Matt] learn more than they ever could have
from a history textbook. Every book in this new series
promises to shed light on a different chapter of
Canadian history."
~ *MONTREAL GAZETTE*

"Readers are in for a great adventure."
~ *EDMONTON'S CHILD*

"This series makes Canadian history fun, exciting
and accessible."
~ *CHRONICLE HERALD (HALIFAX)*

"[An] enthralling series for junior-school readers."
~ *HAMILTON SPECTATOR*

"...highly entertaining, very educational but not too
challenging. A terrific new series."
~ *RESOURCE LINKS*

"This wonderful new Canadian historical adventure series
combines magic and history to whisk young readers away
on adventure...A fun way to learn about Canada's past."
~ *BC PARENT*

"Highly recommended."
~ *CM: CANADIAN REVIEW OF MATERIALS*

Teacher Resource Guides now available online.
Please visit our website at
www.mapletreepress.com/canadianflyeradventures
to download tips and ideas for
using the series in the classroom.

About the Author

Frieda Wishinsky, a former teacher, is an award-winning picture- and chapter-book author, who has written many beloved and bestselling books for children. Frieda enjoys using humour and history in her work, while exploring new ways to tell a story. Her books have earned much critical praise, including a nomination for a Governor General's Award in 1999. In addition to the books in the *Canadian Flyer Adventures* series, Frieda has published *What's the Matter with Albert?*, *A Quest in Time*, and *Manya's Dream* with Maple Tree Press. Frieda lives in Toronto.

About the Illustrator

Gordon Dean Griffiths realized his love for drawing very early in life. At the age of 12, halfway through a comic book, Dean decided that he wanted to become a comic book artist and spent every spare minute of the next few years perfecting his art. In 1995 Dean illustrated his first children's book, *The Patchwork House*, written by Sally Fitz-Gibbon. Since then he has happily illustrated over a dozen other books for young people and is currently working on several more, including the *Canadian Flyer Adventures* series. Dean lives in Duncan, B.C.